The Prince of the Prairie

Betty Selakovich Casey

THE RoadRunner Press
Oklahoma City, Oklahoma

for my parents,
Dan and Beth Selakovich

Published by The RoadRunner Press
Oklahoma City, Oklahoma

Printed in the USA.

Catalog-in-Publication Data is on file at OCLC and SkyRiver and viewable at www.WorldCat.org
Library of Congress Control Number: 2017953500

ISBN: 978-1-937054-72-4
First Edition printed December 2017

10 9 8 7 6 5 4 3 2 1

Once upon a time, a little buffalo lived with his friends Prairie Dog and Meadowlark in a nice green field on the edge of town.

Little Buffalo spent his days running in big circles chasing butterflies. Prairie Dog dozed during the day and dug tunnels at night. Meadowlark could usually be found perched on her favorite branch in a nearby Osage orange tree, singing a song that went like this:

You are the Prince of the Prairie. May you always be merry!
Yes, all was well in their little world on the Great Plains until one day, while watching
the butterflies dance on the wind, Little Buffalo ran into something sharp.

OUCH!

Little Buffalo's cry made Prairie Dog drop his favorite red balloon, the one he always kept safe and sound in his burrow, and scurry to the surface.

Prairie Dog took one look at Little Buffalo and declared, "Do not worry, my friend, I have just the thing for you!"

Little Buffalo thanked his friend for the bandage,

and then he took a good look around the little field.

Little Buffalo did not like what he saw. On every side of his home was a new fence, and just outside each fence was a new house.

Little Buffalo's family had lived in peace and quiet on the prairie, with all the space they needed to roam, for as long as the butterflies had flown.

Now he did not recognize his home.

Little Buffalo could have kicked up his heels and made a stink, but being an accommodating fellow, instead he said, "I will run in smaller circles."

The next day, Little Buffalo woke to find that more houses had popped up overnight, and the butterflies were gone.

When Little Buffalo tried to run in circles, he found that his heart was no longer in it without the butterflies to chase.

Every day, it seemed the houses drew closer, and the fences grew nearer. Now when Little Buffalo went to eat his breakfast, people stopped and watched from their windows.

When Prairie Dog tried to dig a new hole, boys and girls pointed and stared. It was enough to give a shy buffalo and a nocturnal prairie dog a stomachache.

One morning, Little Buffalo woke to find another new house. This one was so close to his fence, he could reach over and touch it.

And so he did.

CRASH!

The noise sent everyone running.

Prairie Dog dived into his burrow.

Meadowlark thought a song might help.

Cheer up! Cheer up!
Prince of the Prairie!

"I do not think he is in the mood, Meadowlark," said Prairie Dog, returning with a bandage for his friend.

The next morning, Little Buffalo woke up hungry and went looking for a crunchy Osage orange and a little song to start his day—only to find that Meadowlark's tree was gone!

"They cut down Meadowlark's tree," Prairie Dog whispered. "The man said they needed the wood to build more houses."

Meadowlark sniffed, "This is too much. It is time to go. Time to go! I shall be building my next nest in the tallgrass prairie."

"What is a tallgrass prairie?" Little Buffalo asked.

"The tallgrass prairie is miles and miles of sweet green grass and wildflowers, butterflies and dragonflies galore, animals and birds as far as the eye can see. The prairie goes on forever and ever to the edge of the sky!" said Meadowlark.

"It sounds beautiful," said Prairie Dog with a wistful sigh.

"It goes on forever and ever?" said Little Buffalo.

"Forever and ever," chirped Meadowlark.

Now Little Buffalo looked wistful too.

"I will miss you, Little Buffalo," Meadowlark said, "and you too, Prairie Dog. It is a shame you two cannot go with me, especially because you, Little Buffalo, are a prince there!"

Little Buffalo looked at the houses creeping in—so close now that he could no longer turn around without touching someone or something. He thought about Meadowlark, who no longer had a branch from which to sing, and Prairie Dog, whose burrow had

been trampled to dust from all the traffic. It felt like a storm was coming, a big storm that would change their little world forevermore. There was only one thing to do. Little Buffalo only hoped it was possible.

"Meadowlark?" Liittle Buffalo said.

"Yes, Little Buffalo?"

"Would you take me with you to the tallgrass prairie, Meadowlark?"

"But of course!" Meadowlark chirped, soaring into the sky with happiness.

"And me!" piped up Prairie Dog.

"Follow me follow me follow me!"
Meadowlark sang.

Looking at the fence, Little Buffalo gulped.

"But how?" Little Buffalo asked.

"Crawl under the fence through my tunnel," suggested Prairie Dog.

So Little Buffalo tried.

When that did not work, Prairie Dog gave Little Buffalo a big push.

PUFFT!

A dirt clod hit Meadowlark in the head. Prairie Dog shook off a coat of dust. Little Buffalo was way too big to use any prairie-dog tunnel.

"Climb over the fence, Little Buffalo," suggested

the nice lady watching from the red house.

So Little Buffalo tried that.

OUCH!

A barb on the barbed-wire fence poked Little Buffalo in his soft belly. He was too tender a buffalo to climb such a fence.

"Fly over the fence," suggested Meadowlark. "Be sure to get a running start."

Being an obliging fellow, Little Buffalo tried that too . . . but to no avail.

SPLAT!

Meadowlark almost fell from the sky as Little Buffalo hit the ground. Prairie Dog took a tumble into his burrow—only to pop back up again with yet another bandage.

"Well, at least you didn't hurt your nose this time," Prairie Dog said.

"It's no use!" Little Buffalo cried. "You two must go without me."

"We would never leave you behind, Little Buffalo!" exclaimed Prairie Dog.

"But I will never get over this fence," cried Little Buffalo.

Prairie Dog jumped up. "I have just the thing!"

And this time it was not a bandage.

"Oh no, not your favorite red balloon!" Little Buffalo said.

"Yes, my red balloon," said Prairie Dog. "It's the only way, my friend."

"Follow me follow me follow me," Meadowlark sang.

And so Little Buffalo did.

It was a magnificent sight to behold.

Little Buffalo landed safely but without the red balloon. As it floated away on the breeze,
Little Buffalo thanked his friend and said, "I am ever so sorry about your balloon."

"It's okay, Little Buffalo," sighed Prairie Dog. "I was saving my balloon for a mighty task.
What could be more mighty than helping you reach your new home?"

"It is just as you said it would be, Meadowlark," Little Buffalo said. "I can see forever and ever, and I have plenty of room to roam and chase butterflies."

"Home sweet home home sweet home," chirped Meadowlark.

"No more bandages for you, Little Buffalo," Prairie Dog said, "but Meadowlark and I have just the thing to take their place!"

"Maybe we should start calling you, Prince," Meadowlark sang.

And with that, Meadowlark broke once more into her favorite song as Prairie Dog placed the small crown on his friend's big head:

You are the Prince of the Prairie. May you always be merry!

And they were. . . .

Just the Facts

Buffalo or bison? The American bison is commonly known as the American buffalo. Although technically not a buffalo, it is part of the family Bovidae, to which the Asian buffalo, African buffalo, and domestic cattle and goats belong. It was early explorers to North America who began to call them buffalo. Bison once numbered in the millions, ranging from northern Canada into Mexico and from coast to coast. If you visit a buffalo preserve, remember that bison can be dangerous—do not leave the car to view them.

Tallgrass Prairie Preserve. The Tallgrass Prairie Preserve in Oklahoma is near the town of Pawhuska in Osage County. At 39,000 acres, it is the largest protected remnant of tallgrass prairie left on earth. It is preserved and protected by The Nature Conservancy, *www.nature.org*.

Prairie. Prairie once covered more than 120 million acres in the United States, including most of Kansas, Nebraska, North Dakota, Oklahoma, and South Dakota as well as portions of Colorado, Illinois, Indiana, Iowa, Minnesota, Missouri, Montana, New Mexico, Wisconsin, and Wyoming. Urban sprawl and conversion to cropland have left less than 10 percent of this magnificent American landscape intact.

Wildlife on the prairie. Oklahoma's Tallgrass Prairie Preserve is home to more than 300 bird and eighty mammal species—from prairie chickens, hawks, and Oklahoma's state bird, the scissor-tailed flycatcher, to golden eagles. Besides bison, you might also see deer, coyotes, and bobcats.

Black-tailed prairie dog. The black-tailed prairie dog makes its home in the Great Plains of North America, from the Canadian border to the Mexican border. Their burrows are used for breeding, rearing young, and hiding from predators.

Western meadowlark. The official state bird of Kansas, the western meadowlark is a ground feeder that lives in grasslands, meadows, and pastures and along marsh edges, according to *allaboutbirds.org*. Western meadowlarks have a flutelike song and build their nests on the ground.

Osage orange. Osage orange is the common name for the bois d'arc tree. It is also known as hedge apple, horse apple, bodark, or dodock. The Osage tribe used wood from the tree to make bows. Pioneers on the plains used the trees for fencing.

Osage pattern. The border on the front cover is based on a pattern used by the Osage tribe in blankets.